*To sons and mommies everywhere...*

ISBN-10: 1532994788
ISBN-13: 978-1532994784

Today is a special day for
mommy and me.

We're going on a special date;
lots of fun things to see!

Daddy makes breakfast
while we pack our lunch.

Sandwiches, and grapes,
and peanuts to munch.

I grab my red cap, and my lucky baseball bat.

Mommy wears a jersey, and a red hat so we'll match.

8

Mommy says she can't wait to watch her little guy play,

And she'll cheer for me loudly at Community Field Day.

We pack up the car, and off we go.

We wave goodbye to daddy with baby sister in tow.

11

We arrive at the park
to an exciting scene!

I see all my friends
from my baseball team.

Kevin, Andrew, Chad, and Zoe,
All hoping to bring home
the big shiny trophy.

Mommy sees friends from the neighborhood too:
My tutor, Mr. Randle, and my school bus driver,
Ms. Sue.

18

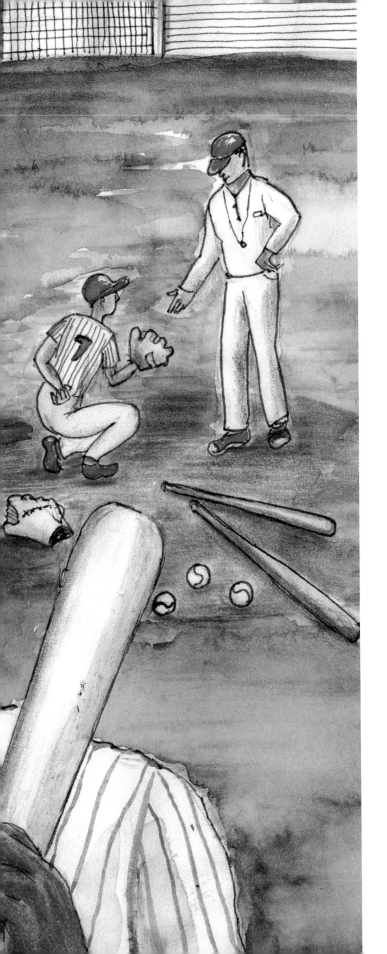

Before the
game begins,
mommy gives
me a big hug,

Then I line up with my team and check in with Coach Doug.

When it's my turn up, I
hurry to the plate with my
bat in hand.

I look up to see mommy
waving proudly in the stands.

I get in my stance and take a hard swing.

I hear a loud crack as the crowd bursts with excited screams!

25

1st, 2nd and even
3rd base!

I run as fast as I
can with a huge
grin on my face.

After the big game,
we gather to eat.

We grab food and
cold drinks to cool
down from the heat.

Mommy holds my hands,
and lets me say grace.
I must be the happiest kid
in the place.

Mommy tells me how proud she is of me,

And how bright my future will surely be.

We laugh, and laugh, and laugh aloud,

'Til mommy and I are the last of the crowd.

We pack up our things along with my first-place prize.

We head for home as the sun leaves the sky.

Today was a perfect day,

Not only because of the winning score.

I tell mommy I love her,

And she tells me she loves me more.

{place keepsake photo here}

# My date with mommy!

An Atlanta, Georgia transplant, Tiffany Bowers is a community development enthusiast and lover of books, imagination, and all things progressive. She holds a BBA in Marketing from Georgia Southern University, and has cultivated a career in the hospitality sales industry, promoting economic growth within the city of Atlanta. She has merged her passion for the community with her passion for writing in a series of children's books geared toward honoring family relationships.

The first in the series, *A Date with Daddy*, highlights a father-daughter interaction through a little girl's eyes as she gets all dressed up and has her first experience on a "date" with her daddy. *A Date with Mommy* follows with a special look at a mother-son relationship as the two celebrate their bond by spending the day at the son's baseball game. An important aspect of developing a thriving community is celebrating and encouraging healthy relationships that instill values and nurture young minds.

Made in the USA
Columbia, SC
11 April 2017